CHARLOTTE AGELL

Dancing Feet

HARCOURT BRACE & COMPANY

Orlando Atlanta Austin Boston San Francisco Chicago Dallas New York
Toronto London

This edition is published by special arrangement with
Harcourt Brace & Company.

Dancing Feet by Charlotte Agell.
Copyright © 1994 by Charlotte Agell.
Reprinted by permission of Harcourt Brace & Company.

Printed in the United States of America

ISBN 0-15-307277-6

2 3 4 5 6 7 8 9 0   026   99 98 97 96

for Peter, Anna, and Jon

Feet, feet

walking down the street,

dancing on the earth,

skipping to the beat.

Hands, hands

digging in the sand,

baking homemade bread,

playing in the band.

Hair, hair

waving in the air,

shining when it's wet,

getting special care.

Arms, arms

pulling with strong tugs,

holding heavy tools,

giving hearty hugs.

Legs, legs

pedaling up and down,

bending at the knee,

strolling through the town.

Eyes, eyes

looking left and right,

crying tears sometimes,

resting through the night.

Mouths, mouths

sipping on a drink,

tasting something new,

saying what they think.

People young and old

doing what they do,

living in the world,

and one of them is you!